THIS CANDLEWICK BOOK BELONGS TO:

_____

_____

_____

For Audrey and David

First U.S. paperback edition 2007

The Library of Congress has cataloged the hardcover edition as follows:
Dale, Penny.
Princess, princess / Penny Dale.
p. cm.
Summary: A young princess and her friends sleep under the spell of a fairy she forgot
to invite to her birthday party, until someone comes along to awaken them.
ISBN 978-0-7636-2212-1 [hardcover]
[1. Princesses—Fiction. 2. Fairies—Fiction. 3. Sleep—Fiction. 4. Fairy tales.] I. Title.
PZ7.D1525Pr 2003
[E]—dc21   2002041112

ISBN 978-0-7636-3565-7 [paperback]

2 4 6 8 10 9 7 5 3 1

Printed in China

This book was typeset in GoudyHundred.
The illustrations were done in watercolor and colored pencil.

Candlewick Press
2067 Massachusetts Avenue
Cambridge, Massachusetts 02140

visit us at www.candlewick.com

Princess, Princess

Penny Dale

CANDLEWICK PRESS
CAMBRIDGE, MASSACHUSETTS

There's a princess in a castle, sleeping, sleeping,
surrounded by her best friends, sleeping, sleeping.

For the longest time they've all been sleeping, sleeping.
Who will wake the princess with a kiss?

Once the princess spent her days
playing, playing,
dancing through the castle,
running, singing.

Riding on her horse,
playing in the garden,
playing with her best friends,
hiding, chasing.

Until one day the princess asked the fairies
to a party in the castle, her birthday party.

So they all came flitting, flying, bringing presents,
and everyone was happy to be there.

Except this frowning little fairy
whom the princess forgot to ask,
but still she came.
And when she saw the princess
playing without her,
what she wanted was to spoil the fun,
to spoil the game.

"Sleep, princess, sleep! Now all your games are over!"
The little fairy cast a spell.

"Sleep, sleep, with all your friends around you!
Sleep, sleep, until you're woken with a kiss!"

So the princess in the castle fell to sleeping,
surrounded by her best friends, sleeping, sleeping.

For the longest time they've all been sleeping, sleeping.
Who will wake the princess with a kiss?

For the longest time a forest has been growing
around the castle, full of dreams, full of shadows.

There are no ways, no paths toward the castle.
Who will wake the princess with a kiss?

Who is flitting, flying through the shadows?
Who is flitting, flying through the trees?

Who is flitting, flying through the forest?
Who will wake the princess with a kiss?

The little fairy, sorry for her anger,
comes back at last
to break the sleeping spell.
Not frowning now,
but smiling, gently smiling . . .

The little fairy wakes

the princess with a kiss.

There's a princess in a castle, playing, playing, running, dancing, singing with her friends.

Skipping through the garden with a little fairy,
happy princess, happy fairy, happy friends.

Penny Dale is the author-illustrator of numerous acclaimed books for children, including *Ten in the Bed* and *The Boy on the Bus: A Sing-Along Storybook*. She is also the illustrator of *The Jamie and Angus Stories* by Anne Fine. Of this book, she says, "I very much enjoyed reworking the story of Sleeping Beauty with the children center stage — playing out the drama in their own way." Penny Dale lives in Wales.